Dare You?

Dare or Danger

by

Sue Graves

Illustrated by Aleksandar Sotirovski

First published in 2009 in Great Britain by
Barrington Stoke Ltd
18 Walker St, Edinburgh, EH3 7LP

www.barringtonstoke.co.uk

Title ISBN: 978-1-84299-713-0
Pack ISBN: 978-1-84299-787-1

Printed in Great Britain by The Charlesworth Group

We dare the author to answer the question ...

What's the most embarrassing thing that's ever happened to you?

Probably the most embarrassing thing that's ever happened to me was when I was learning to ski. On the first lesson I was carrying my skis on my shoulder up a steep slope when I dropped them. The skis slid down the hill and knocked over my ski instructor who was following behind. He wasn't very pleased at all! I'm sure he thought I was the worst pupil ever.

For Isabelle and William

It was time for lunch. Mick, the school bully, and his mates were fed up. Mick saw Dan and Lee messing around with the coin they had found in the woods.

"Come on," Mick said to his mates.

"Let's have some fun with Dan and Lee."

Mick pushed Lee just as he was tossing the coin in the air. The coin hummed and landed on the ground. It said **dare**.

Mick grabbed the coin and looked at it.

3

"**Dare**," said Mick. He nodded his head slowly. Just then, he saw Max eating his lunch.

"I dare you to grab Mad Max's lunch," he said. "Then you can have your coin back."

Lee and Dan looked at each other and gulped. Everyone called him 'Mad Max' because of his bad temper. No one messed with him!

"Let's do it," said Lee. "Come on Dan."

The boys ran over to Max.

"Your teacher, Mr Hill, wants to see you," said Lee.

"What?" grunted Max.

"He says you must go now," said Dan.

Max went inside. The boys grabbed his
lunch. They took it to Mick.

"Now you give us the coin," Lee said to Mick.

"Not till you've done another dare," said Mick. He grabbed Lee's bag and threw it on to the school roof. "Dare you to get that."

"Only if you come with me," said Lee.

"Dare you, Mick?" his mates asked.

"You bet I dare!" said Mick. "I'm cool!"

Lee and Mick climbed on to the roof.

Lots of kids watched them.

Lee got hold of the bag and got down from the roof. But Mick slipped. He slid down the roof and got hooked up by his trousers on the top of the drainpipe.

"Help!" yelled Mick. "I'm stuck!"

Fred, the care-taker, went and got a ladder and helped Mick down.

Then Mick saw that everyone was
pointing at him and laughing.

He felt the back of his trousers. There was a big hole in them and everyone could see his sad pants. Mick went very red.

"You think you're cool," laughed Lee.
"But your pants are not!"

DARE OR DANGER

Watch out for more **Dare or Danger** books coming soon ...

Up in Flames

The coin shows Danger.

There's a fire and someone's life is in danger ... can the boys come to the rescue?

Doom Ride

The coin shows Dare.

Lee and Dan dare to take on Doom Ride – the scariest ride in the theme park. But even they aren't prepared for what happens next ...

For more info check out our website:
www.barringtonstoke.co.uk